TEXTING
Smash-Ups, Mishaps, and Laughs

Gail Galvan

TEXTING: Smash-Ups, Mishaps, and Laughs

Copyright © 2016 Gail (Davis) Galvan

Cover Design by Gail Galvan
and CreateSpace/Thank you!

Interior graphics by clker.com/Thank you!

All rights reserved.

This is a work of fiction. Names, characters, businesses, places, events and incidents are either the products of the author's imagination or used in a fictitious manner. Any resemblance to actual persons, living or dead, or actual events in relation to texting tragedies and/or mishaps is purely coincidental.

Author's Note: A portion of proceeds from this book (one dollar per copy sold) will be donated to The National Safety Council to help raise awareness regarding texting distraction.

ISBN-13: 978-1523424351

ISBN-10: 1523424354

Printed in the United States of America

(Note: If purchased other than in the U.S, copies may be printed elsewhere.)

DEDICATION

To whom it may concern—
which is all of us

and

For the preventers

CONTENTS

INTRODUCTION

PART ONE: On the Darker Side

PART TWO: On the Lighter Side

PART THREE: On the Contemplative Side

INTRODUCTION

CALLS KILL.

WATCH THE VIDEOS ON-LINE

https://www.youtube.com/watch?v=R0LCmStIw9E

http://www.bing.com/videos/search?q=video+texting+while+driving+youtube&&view

http://www.nsc.org/learn/NSC-Initiatives/Pages/distracted-driving.aspx?var=-1'

Horrific videos regarding distracted driving
are more profoundly effective than a thousand words
or devastating statistics.

Please pledge allegiance
to yourself and others
to drive safely.

GOD'S SPEED.

PART ONE: ON THE DARKER SIDE

Headlines

Hell Hospital

Last Words

When I Grow Up

HEADLINES

"EXTRA! EXTRA! READ ALL ABOUT IT!"

DISTRACTED DAYS IN HISTORY

Texting Disrupts, Maims, and Kills

In Denver, Colorado, there was a 13 pile-up car crash on I-25. Three were killed. Many others were critically injured and will spend years trying to recover. One lady miscarried. Several were burnt badly. Two people are now blind. Three victims will never walk again. There was no doubt that the tragic incident was caused by texting and driving. It took weeks, but finally one teen in the car that caused the crash revealed that she had just begged her friend to put down the phone, quit texting with one hand, and just drive. Her friend laughed. Two minutes later, the deadly chaos began.

In Indianapolis, Indiana two teenage girls were coming home from playing in a basketball game and died when a car collided with them head on. The driver of the other car lived and admitted to texting. "I just took my eyes off the road for a second."

While a woman was walking her six year old daughter to school in Lexington, Kentucky, a man texting drove up onto the sidewalk and ran over the little girl. She died. The grieving mother planted a garden in her backyard with crosses to memorialize her daughter. Mrs. Kelter swears that she will kill the man who killed her adorable Samantha, someday.

In San Diego, California, in a parking lot by an ocean beach, two teenage boys were lifting their surfboards out of the convertible when another teen driver, who was texting, plowed into the boys and crushed them both—to death.

Texting: Smash-Ups, Mishaps, and Laughs

While vacationing in Hawaii, an elderly couple planned to celebrate their 50th wedding anniversary, but their lives came to an abrupt tragic halt when a distracted texting driver crashed into them as they drove to the restaurant. Family and friends had to plan their unexpected funeral instead of celebrate their fifty years together.

50 YEARS   50 YEARS

In Dallas Texas, after a football game, two young adult fans were driving to a bar to celebrate the win, but they crashed into a semi-truck instead as the driver texted to another friend where they were headed. The driver lives with guilt, drug addiction, only one arm, and a head injury now, and probably for the rest of her life. Her best friend, Tara, died in the car crash that awful day.

In Tulsa, Oklahoma, a young girl named MaryLyn was walking her beloved 5 year old pet, Sally, a German shepherd. When a texting driver failed to stop at a light, the girl and dog were hit. MaryLyn cradled her pet's body in her arms—feeling a part of her die, too—as Sally took her last breath. MaryLyn's T-shirt, that she wore that day read: THIS GIRL LOVES HER GERMAN SHEPHERD.

A ten year old girl was shopping at a local mall in Hartford, Connecticut. She got on an escalator, started texting, made some sort of misstep, tumbled down and broke her neck. After four weeks on a ventilator and other life support measures, the devastated, bereaved young parents pulled the plug. On their daughter, Haley's behalf—the parents now travel all over the country and speak in schools about tragic statistics and safe texting to try and prevent more tragedies like theirs. They call it the T.L.C. Awareness Talk: Texting, Living with Consequences. They pray every day that they can make a difference and prevent texting tragedies, so their daughter's death is not endured in vain.

Texting: Smash-Ups, Mishaps, and Laughs

(Scranton, North Dakota) "Who names a cat Catnip anyway, that's just stupid?" the 14 year old boy asked in his nasal, whiny voice.

"Yeah, well I'll tell you what's stupid, Nicholas—and cruel—is for you to stomp all over my poor kitty's hind leg. I told you the vet said he almost had to amputate it, and you didn't ever even say you're sorry," Kelly complained.

"Well, it's always right there at a person's feet, what am I supposed to do—jump over it every time?"

"No, you're supposed to put your stupid phone down and stop texting while you're walking. I heard about you tripping over the chair the other day and almost crashing into the TV. You never pay attention! It cost me $300 dollars at the vet, by the way, and I think you should pay for it…and another thing…if we did have to amputate, I'd amputate you!" Kelly knew it was useless and turned to walk away.

"Oh, all right, all right. I'm sorry. I'll be more careful. But I don't have $300 and Catnip's still a stupid name for a cat."

HELL HOSPITAL

"What do you mean transported? Where the hell am I? How do I get out of this hell hole?" Paul asked the long blond-haired teenage girl sitting beside him. He darted his eyes here and there to try and take in all he was seeing. "It's all black and white in here. Everything in this room—and what's with the devil heads, pitchforks, and NO TEXTING poster wallpaper all over?"

"Jesus, stop! How many questions can a girl answer at once, mister?" She took a puff off of a straw. "Let's see…just what I said, transported. This is Hell Hospital and you're in it. There ain't no way out, not for a year anyway, until you've served you're sentence and changed that stinky attitude of yours. You're sick, I'm sick, supposedly, we're all sick, all of us scoundrels….the only cure here is to learn the evils of texting while driving. Jeez, and how do I know why there's no friggen color in this hell hole joint…wish I had a joint, you got any buddha on you? Anything 'sa-weet' in your pockets?" She ran her slender fingers through her hair and took another puff off of her make-believe cigarette.

"Is that straw really doing it for you? How much nicotine is there in a straw anyway, cutie?"

"Don't call me cutie. My name's Dar Lisa and you're name is mud, 'cause like I said, you're stuck here along with the rest of us." Instead of laughing, she just stared at Paul awaiting the fear to erupt from within his brain.

"So like....prisoners, you mean? I'm only 24 years old and I'm a prisoner?"

"Yeah, buddy, now you got it. You killed three people, right? What do you think, they give a texting murderous idiot an Academy Award? You should get three awards then. Me? I only get one. They say it's my fault this old lady died and all because she had a bad ticker. Her granddaughter says me crossing over, heading for their car, gave her granny a heart attack at the wheel. Just 'cause she had a bad ticker, I'm stuck down here…It's like they say, life just ain't fair." This time she smiled and laughed wickedly while tapping him on the right shoulder. "I'll tell you what. Why don't you go out that door there, down the hallway, and get one of the nurses at the Nurses' Station to help you out." She pointed toward the stark white door.

"That's just what I'll do, by God. And I didn't kill anybody on purpose. It was just one of those things. Could happen to anybody." His six-foot tall body ran out the door and down the long hallway. He saw figures at what seemed to be a Nurses' Station. The white uniforms and old-time nursing hats gave him hope.

As he got closer, though, his heart started racing even faster and he jolted into a panic mode. None of the nurses had faces—complete blanks—no eyes, no noses, no mouths so somebody could tell him what the hell was going on. Most importantly, how he could stop it all and return to his good life as a computer analyst back in Portland, Oregon.

"I'm in a friggen twilight zone. Oh God, please help me. Wizard man, I wanna go home. Please God…I really want to go home now." He ran back to the room where he had talked with the girl, but she was gone. So back down the hallway, he took a closer look at the mannequin-like nurses and saw huge buttons running down the front of their uniforms. A sign at the desk read: *Push the top button for instructions to proceed.* His hand shook violently, but he pushed at it and heard a click, then a caring, clear voice.

"Continue on down this hallway, turn right and enter the room with a door marked A." He took some long deep breaths trying to calm himself down, then bolted down the hallway. He entered the A-Room and saw nine people sitting in chairs formed in a circle. The blond-haired girl was among them. She motioned for him to sit down beside her.

"Thanks a lot for the help," he said sarcastically.

"No problem. Now shut up and listen. My name is Dar Lisa, I'm a text addict. I'm here, I guess, because I caused the death of some old lady with a bad heart. The police put it all on me, but it was raining, too, and that could have been a part of it all. I don't know. I'm trying to take responsibility, but it's hard and I want out of this HELL HOLE!" She screamed the last two words.

The middle-aged lady on her right began to talk next. "My name is Rosemary and I'm a text addict.

Texting: Smash-Ups, Mishaps, and Laughs

I'm here because I caused the death of a mom and her 4 year old daughter. I was just trying to text my husband real quick, to remind him that I had a dental appointment in the afternoon and he would have to take off work and drive me home. Before I knew it, I crashed into the car in front of me. Their stupid car was a lightweight and mine's a tank, a Ford Queen Victoria. So, of course, my car barreled down on the other lady's car and that was it. My life is over, well, theirs too….but mine, too."

And so it went—all tragic deaths, all caused by texting, a driver who was distracted and not paying attention.

When it came time for Paul to speak, he just sat there, swallowed hard, fidgeted endlessly, and asked for a glass of water.

"No, no water. No food. We eat, drink once a day. You missed it by getting here after three p.m. You have to share or you'll be here without food and water until you do. If you talk, you'll get to at least sleep on a bed tonight in a ten by five foot cell. So fess up, Mister," the blond-haired girl with a pretty name urged him.

After a long silence and looks that could kill—as easily as a distracted texting driver—he told the others like it was.

"All right, all right. My freakin' name is Paul Sanders, and I screwed up. I was driving and wanted to text my girlfriend to tell her to meet me. I was gonna give her a key to my apartment. I told her to meet me at my mom's house. But she had forgotten the address; she'd only been there once before. So I went to type in the street number...and honest to God, that's all I remember. Next thing I know, I was lying in a hospital bed with this gash in my forehead and blood all over my right arm. My mom was there and told me the gruesome news. She said, 'Son, I don't know how or when, but you will learn to live with this. People saw you texting. There was a crash. Three people are dead because of you. Oh son, how many times? How many times did I warn you, my dear son?' Then my mom just freaked out and started praying crazy-like over my body."

And so, the new prisoner got his orientation. The next day, he pushed a second button on another still-life nurse. It assigned him to Room B where he

Texting: Smash-Ups, Mishaps, and Laughs

would choose the skills that he would learn.

He had choices. He would serve an internship and assist in one of the following professions: a Plastic Surgery Clinic, Burn Unit, or Grief Center. He was warned that the Grief Center was the toughest, because parts of bodies might be able to be improved, repaired to a certain degree, but the mind—nobody was ever certain about the mind, how much healing could be done or how much damage seemed to always remain, no matter what.

Failure, bad attitudes, unwillingness to accept responsibility, if these were the results of his presence, then it simply and ultimately meant eternity in hell. No way out, ever. If prisoners managed to get back to their lives and texted again while driving, once again—ZAP—eternity in hell it would be.

Mister Sanders seemed to be making progress. He dealt with his consequences, showed remorse, and learned some skills. Once he got back to his life, he worked at a Burn Unit. But on the way home one day, he heard the music—Pearl Jam—which meant his cell had just gone off. He wanted to know if he had gotten a promotion, if he could cut his hours at the Burn Clinic and go back to his other job. Paul had always kept the cell phone safely in the glove compartment to remind him that hell awaited him again if he weakened at any point in time.

Who knows why people do things when they know what the dire consequences will be? Hell hath no fury as it does with those weak or determined enough to choose eternity by repeating the same mistakes. Paul mumbled, "Ah, hell with it," leaned over and reached to open the glove compartment, got the phone out, answered it, and crashed into the car in front of him. One more fatal statistic to add to the disastrous count.

Paul's mother stood in the hallway hospital after seeing her son, suddenly dropped to her knees, flung open her purse and desperately opened a zippered compartment, took out a nitroglycerin pill, and popped it under her tongue. She held onto her chest and felt as if her heart would flop out onto the floor if she didn't press against it and hold it in.

She sat down, pushed herself up against a wall and veered back at the hospital unit she had just come from. For six months now, Paul had remained mostly

Texting: Smash-Ups, Mishaps, and Laughs

in a coma, yet one day he had actually regained consciousness briefly at one point and mumbled something about a blond-haired girl and being a prisoner, doing penance. He also whispered in his mom's ear—that one miraculous day—that he wanted to live in the olden days when there were no telephones or cars, just horses, buggies, and telegraph offices. Then he had slipped back into the coma death-like silence again.

As Mrs. Sanders regained her strength and walked away, the grieving mother looked back again and read the sign above the unit's entrance doorway: *Chicago Cook County Hospital Coma and Near-Death Life Experience Unit.*

LAST WORDS

"Oh, God, no! Oh, Lord, no…no…no…no…no!" Gina screamed as she gripped the steering wheel as tightly as she could.

"Yeah, Sis, we're going over. This is it; I love you." Kelsey said in tears and with a crackly, but oddly calm, voice to her big sister. She raised her left arm and placed her hand on Gina's shoulder.

"Oh God, Sis, let's pray. Our Father who art in…no wait, first…I'm so sorry Kelsey. Bye to my sweet cats, brothers, friends, and Thomas. No grandmas for us, after all. I love you. Bye." She grabbed Kelsey's hand off her shoulder and squeezed. Both of them closed their eyes at this point…as time seemed to stand still while they continued to fly through the air. The only problem was the fact that—cars don't fly.

"Thy kingdom come, thy will be…." Their last words.

CRASH! The Ford Focus had bolted forward and upward off of the edge of the road into the sky. Then came the crashing down as the front end collided with the hill, all the rocks, dirt. It rolled over five times until it finally came to a jerky deadly stop.

Onlookers and helpers above had already begun to gather at the edge of the road, descend and try to reach the victims. Everyone rushed and hoped but—to no avail.

No lingering last breaths, just a sudden halt for both Gina and Kelsey. No chances for recovery or years of rehabilitation with hopes of returning to some semblance of a quality life. It all ended there—off of route 4 near Clancy, Illinois.

TWO HOURS BEFORE THE CRASH

A wonderful, fun day was about to begin. "You wanna try and walk the mall today, Kels?" Kelsey was still recovering from surgery to repair a herniated disc in her back. Yet she yearned for the exercise and knew she needed it. With her shiny blue cane, she planned to walk the whole mall.

Slowly but surely, the two of them made it from Sears to Penny's on the top level, then took the escalator down and walked in reverse on the lower level of the Swan Lake Mall in Merrillville, Indiana.

They mostly window shopped, but did buy something at the As Seen On TV store. Kelsey wanted to see if that Egg-Tastic oval-shaped invention worked to produce fluffy scrambled eggs quickly in the microwave. Gina bought a couple pairs of cheap earrings from Claire's. A big debate took place before they decided to dine at the Olive Garden restaurant just outside of the mall rather than at the Food Court.

It was just after noon and the play did not start until 2:30 p.m. so they took their time at lunch.

"Yum, I gotta have me some more of that salad and delicious dressing. I love this dressing." She dished out some more salad on her plate. "You want some more breadsticks, Sis?"

"Yeah, sure. Well, maybe no. New Year, same old resolution, another try. I'm gonna have some more soup."

"Okay, me too. We'll skip the breadsticks and butter." She waved at their waitress and both took a drink of water. After water and soup refills, the conversation started up again. "So I can't believe we're going to be grandmas, finally. Well, me, an auntie-granny anyway. You think about two more weeks for Kerrie? She looks ready now!"

"That's what she said, so guess we can wait that long; then we'll get our little guy to spoil." Gina took Kelsey's hand and squeezed it. Smiling she said, "I never thought it would happen, did you?"

"Nope, not with Thomas taking his sweet time and always saying: 'No kids, Mom, no kids.' Thought I was out of luck for sure, but my son finally came through for us, how about that?" They both laughed.

Gina kept checking her watch. When they couldn't take in another bite, lunch time was over. They hopped in the car and headed for the theatre.

With a little time to kill before the play started, they wandered around in the Art Gallery at the theatre admiring the stunning black and white photographs by Ansel Adams. His masterpieces included amazing images: the Dunes, Yosemite, the Grand Canyon, Mexican adobe structures, cliffs, just so many striking black and white artistic lines that mesmerize.

Texting: Smash-Ups, Mishaps, and Laughs

At 2:20 p.m., Gina and Kelsey took their seats to see *The Signal*. Kelsey nudged her sister. "This is so cool. Thanks for the ticket." Gina always got season tickets to the Classic Theatre.

Before the play started Kelsey and Gina read the programs that were handed out. "I don't remember the Spaniels, do you Gina?"

"Nope. I remember this song, though, they mention here, 'Goodnight Sweetheart, Goodnight.' " She glanced down at the program and pointed, so Kelsey could see it. "This history sounds so fascinating, especially since we grew up in Gary, too. Just think, down on 17th and Broadway, downtown, all of this musical magic was going on in 1956. Well, I was only three and you weren't even born yet. Of course we know about the Jacksons and Stormy Weather, but Willie Rogers, The Spaniels, Pookie Hudson, this deejay lady, Vivian Carter, her Vee-Jay records, and this one dude telling the story, Henry Farag, I never heard of any of them. Have you, Sis?"

She turned to Kelsey, just as the lights dimmed. Kelsey whispered to answer, "No, never heard of any of them. We'll have to research it on the net when we get home….Shhh….Here we go. I know we're in for some great music."

The Doo Wop Rhapsody of "In the Still of the Night" led the way. One harmonious melody after another serenaded the audience, got them clapping, and dancing in their hearts. The story and music took them all back to an amazing, unforgettable era in history—especially for those who grew up in "the Region," Northwest, Indiana.

The finale clamored on with clapping, hollering, whistles, a couple encore songs, and a standing ovation. Outside the theatre, while leaving, Gina and Kelsey complimented the singers and shook their hands.

Back at the car, Kelsey said, "I'm so glad I got out and decided to come with you. I mean that was really cool."

"Yeah, it was…I love that kind of music!"

"Me too."

"Hey, you want to hear some Adele on the way home? I just bought her CD, it's pretty good." Gina fidgeted with the radio and CD and got it to play. "Didn't you say that Kerrie and Thomas picked out a name for the baby the other day?"

"Yeah, I did. But you won't like it?"

"Why, what is it?" Gina asked and drove off.

"Sonny or Frankie, they said."

"What kind of name is that? They think our family has a Mafia bloodline or something? Whatever happened to Paul or John, or whatever?"

"Don't ask me…I know, what a lame name. Maybe you can persuade them to change it."

As Adele sang her heart out, the tune "Rollin' in the Deep," Kelsey noticed the driver to the right of her. "Hey, Gina, look at this girl one car up, the blue Suburban, she's texting a way as she's driving. She's got kids in the car, too. I just saw another driver too, a guy, talking on the phone. I thought things were changing. Guess not."

Gina stopped for a light. "I'll get in the right hand lane and stay back a little. I don't trust her."

"Okay, Sis, so what are you doing tomorrow?"

"Oh, I don't know, probably go visit Mom and Dad."

In the next instant, Gina slammed on the brakes because everyone in front of her was slamming on the brakes, too. She just knew she'd kill the family in front of her if she didn't swerve to try and avoid them.

Another horrifying, senseless day in texting distraction history added to the fatal statistics. Five dead, six critically injured, and, of course, the girl who texted while driving, the one many witnesses say caused it all, walked away with minor injuries. For so many others, luck had run out.

Gina and Kelsey were among the dead. They never would enjoy being a grandma or living out the rest of their lives.

These were their last words.

"Oh, God, no! Oh, Lord, no…no…no…no… no!" Gina screamed as she gripped the steering wheel as tightly as she could.

"Yeah, Sis, we're going over. This is it; I love you." Kelsey said in tears and with a crackly, but oddly calm, voice to her big sister. She raised her left arm and placed her hand on Gina's shoulder.

"Oh God, Sis, let's pray. Our Father who art in…no wait, first…I'm so sorry Kelsey. Bye to my sweet cats, brothers, friends, and Thomas. No grandmas for us, after all. I love you. Bye." She grabbed Kelsey's hand off her shoulder and squeezed. Both of them closed their eyes at this point...as time seemed to stand still while they continued to fly through the air. The only problem was the fact that—cars don't fly.

"Thy kingdom come, thy will be..." Their last words.

WHEN I GROW UP

"Mom, when I grow up, is it okay if I don't become a waitress like you? I wanna be an actress like Dakota Fanning or Julia Roberts or Sandra Bullock." Sara tugged at her hair tie to loosen her ponytail. "And will you put my hair in pigtails today, please, please, please?" She handed her mother a brush.

"Well of course, Sara Marie, you can be anything you want to be. Your dad and I always tell you that."

They sat down at the dining room table while two perfect pigtails were brushed and tied into place with two blue ribbons.

"I know, but you get all those tips, I wanna make as much money as you!"

"Oh I'm sure as an actress, a successful one, anyway, you'll make lots more than a waitress makes." She laughed at her daughter's naiveté.

"Good, 'cause I'm pretty sure I'm gonna start my acting career in March when our school puts on the Easter play, *New Jack Rabbit City*. There's an eight year old girl named Abby in it and it's the main part and I'd get to sing and everything."

"Really. This is the first I've heard of this, but good for you." Her mom gave her a quick hug.

"Yep, Exna is sick, she's got pneumonia, so she can't try out and she's the only other singer better than me in choir." Sara Marie held up a small mirror. "Oh thanks, Mommy, I love it. I just can't get them good like you do."

"I love it when you still call me Mommy sometimes even though you're such a grown up little eight year old actress. There you go, now off to school." They both stood up, Sara grabbed her coat and backpack, and after another mom-daughter hug and "I love you" she left to walk the six blocks to George Kuny School.

At supper that evening she told her mom and dad the "most amazing, most absolutely fabulous news."

She said, "Well, you're looking at the next Dakota Fanning, or maybe even Elle Fanning, I like 'em both. I got the part, Mom."

Dave looked at Ruth and asked, "What's this all about?" He offered everyone else the mashed potatoes, then put some more on his plate.

"Well, apparently, our daughter is going to be an actress and star in her school play at Easter time." Sara's brother Lenny rolled his eyes and her other brother did the same thing. Shannon, Sara's three year old sister, mimicked her brothers and rolled her eyes, too.

"Oh you guys, just wait, you'll see. Just 'cause you don't have any talent. I can't help that." She poked Lenny and Larry in the shoulder.

"Mom!" They both yelled. "Yeah, right, you forget I'm shortstop now for two years and Larry is, oh what's that called in sports, oh yeah, quarterback." Lenny pinched Sara on the leg.

"Ouch! Mom, Dad, he just pinched me. Brat!"

"All right, already, stop. Eat your supper, and congratulations to all of our talented kids. What's the play about Sara?" her dad asked.

"All I know is that rabbits drink magic water, grow tall and they can talk! And, Abby, the little girl I'll play, she gets to sing songs in the play. There's this one I heard today already. It's called 'I Believe in Magic.' It's so pretty. I can't wait!"

"Well that's great sweetie, good for you." Her dad said while both her mom and dad smiled and looked at each other.

Both brothers continued with the eye rolls and smirks on their faces. Although Sara Marie was actually a very good tomboy and sports player—they thought her love for plays was just silly, especially musicals, the way the actors just started blurting out a song all of a sudden. They wouldn't be going to any stupid play if they could help it.

Four weeks later, Sara walked around bursting with excitement. She was living a dream and just knew she'd be starring in a movie someday and fans would be asking for *her* autograph and for sure an Academy Award awaited her one fantastic day in the future as a young movie star.

The second evening of the play, the director told Sara and her parents the good news. Gary Music Theatre wanted to put on the production, too. *New Jack Rabbit City* would be presented on the big stage one year later before Easter, and Sara was first in line to play the part.

Capital letters and hearts and exclamation

marks filled Sara's diary later that day.

"Mom, can I take Duke for a short walk just before supper?" She grabbed the leash from off the hook on the wall by the door.

"Sure, you've got about a half hour. Make sure you're back in time." Her mom pulled out a frying pan from the oven.

"Okay, Mom, bye."

"C'mon, boy, let's go to the lake." She petted Duke on top of his head and hooked the leash to his collar.

"Guess what, Duke, you're looking at a movie star. Yep, that's me, SARA MARIE, in big letters, probably in the movies—and on Broadway. I'll be on late shows and everything. I sure wish David Letterman was still around, you know, since he's a guy from Indiana and I'm a girl from Indiana." She started singing the main theme song from the play as she wandered down the tracks toward Lake Robinson with her Marmaduke-looking, furry best friend.

"I believe in magic now, I believe, I believe. Can't tell me it doesn't happen, just believe, just believe. I believe in magic now, I believe, I believe.

Can't tell me it doesn't happen, just believe, just believe."

Later that evening after supper and helping with the dishes, Sara Marie and her brother Lenny planned to play some baseball at the open field down the street. Of course Sara had to beg her big brother to take her, but he finally agreed. After all, Sara was just as good as any boy on the team. Sara said she wanted to ride her bike for a little bit, but she told him she would be there.

Before she left, she told her mom, yet again, that she was going to be an actress when she grew up and just how happy she was going to be. Most of all, she wanted to meet the Fanning sisters someday or even, maybe, star in a movie with one of them.

Three minutes later....that's where this story twists around toward an unfathomable darkness and unbearably painful kill-joy tale.

No ballgame that night. No singing young acting star on the auditorium stage at George Kuny grade school the next day. No future, whatsoever, for a bright, talented, lively, incredibly sweet, loving eight year old girl named Sara Marie.

Texting: Smash-Ups, Mishaps, and Laughs

One minute—the liveliest, most precious heartbeat a child could ever possess—the next minute, silence. The kind of heart wrenching silence that would mean nothing would ever be the same or anything the future was ever supposed to be.

A sixteen year old neighbor, a friendly girl from the Harrison family who lived down the street from Sara, had just gotten her license two weeks ago. Mallory was coming home from soccer practice at school. She heard her phone, picked it up, began to text some kind of unimportant message to one of her girlfriends. At that very moment her car swerved to the right and smashed into Sara and her bike. Mallory slammed on the brakes, but all of the ugliest, devastating, unforgettable image-type damage in the world someone can imagine had just occurred.

Mallory got out and collapsed to the ground. She knew the little neighbor girl was dead and that she—NO…TEXTING WHILE DRIVING—had just killed her.

Bike helmets don't help when a ninety pound bicyclist gets run over. Internal injuries were the physical cause of death.

The show did go on, about two weeks later at Sara's grade school, just one more time, in honor of Sara Marie Davidson….with the understudy, now, of course, taking the young star's place.

The Davidson family found it in their hearts to forgive Mallory, but the stolen joy from that happy household eats away at the members every day.

Mallory, now 21 years old, did the usual after the horrifying fatal incident and continues to do so once a week—attends presentations about the madness and sadness that evolves around distracted drivers and always zooms in on the dangers of texting while at the wheel.

Sara's brother, Lenny, walks Duke down the tracks to the lake at times. Suppertime and life goes on at the Davidson's, but none of it—none of it—is the same as when their lively, loving, smiling Sara Marie was around.

PART TWO: ON THE LIGHTER SIDE

Headlines

The Manning Brothers:
Goofy Golfing Guys

Withdrawal is the Worst

Obsessive-Compulsive? Who Me?

All Bruised Up

Sociologically Speaking

Can't Kill a Dreamer on Two Wheels

HEADLINES

"EXTRA! EXTRA! READ ALL ABOUT IT!"

DISTRACTED DAYS IN HISTORY

Texting: Distracted Moments Create Comedy at Times

A lifeguard witnessed a fully clothed lady fall into the pool at the Y.M.C.A. as she walked along toward the edge of the pool. "I tried to get her attention. Must have been a parent of one of the kids swimming. She slipped and that was it, SPASH! I saw her texting and walking too close to the water. Then she just slipped. Not only that, but she kept holding her phone up high, trying to make sure it didn't get wet. That's what she seemed most worried about. You never heard such laughter from everyone there!"

Daily Newspaper Article/Los Angeles

A Golden Dream
by
Reporter Percy Varrants

(Author's note: Characters in this story are based on *The Golden Girls*, however, names were changed.)

"Picture it." Betty White, the beloved funny golden girl is hosting *Saturday Night Live* once again. She tells this hilarious bit about a dream she says she really did have one summer night while living in her L.A. home. Betty says the dream felt as if she was living out a real rehearsal or episode for *The Golden Girls* TV show. The adorable, ever-so-youth-like comedienne stood before the live audience and told a story that made us laugh just as she did so many other times in her amazing career.

"It was a Christmas episode because presents were scattered about and I was holding a snow-globe and a cell phone, of all things, showing it to the other girls as we sat around in the living room. Then all of a sudden, well, you know how dreams just switch around all over the place, I hear Dahpney yelling, but we're all out on the lanai now."

"Ma! Ma! Oh God, girls, you've got to help me. Ma's gone…She's taken the phone book and a couch

Texting: Smash-Ups, Mishaps, and Laughs

cushion, MY CAR…AND her cell phone….You know she got that ticket just the other day for driving with a forty year old expired license and TEXTING as she pulled up to a stop sign…girls, I'm afraid she's gonna kill herself or some innocent person."

"Well, for some reason, Barb and I just ignore Daphney and don't say a word, because we're both on our cell phones, too. Then we hear Sylvia walk through the door, and sure enough she's carrying a phone book, a couch cushion, she has her purse, and a cell phone. So what happens next, you want to know, do you? Well, of course you do. Cheesecake! We're all sitting around at our small kitchen table in our silky pajama outfits eating cheesecake and, well, you know me, I start reciting some crazy St. Olaf story. But the girls weren't listening, anyway. No, they were all texting on their cell phones…even Sylvia. I got so mad. I just ate another piece of cheesecake, and that made everything all right."

What a way to start the night—hey, *Saturday Night Live* fans? Gotta love her, just gotta love her. May we all celebrate your joy, Betty White, golden girl, when that 95th birthday comes around.

The Golden Girls is an American sitcom created by Susan Harris that originally aired on NBC from September 14, 1985, to May 9, 1992. The series starred Beatrice Arthur, Betty White, Rue McClanahan, and Estelle Getty. It was produced by Witt/Thomas/Harris Productions, in association with Touchstone Television, and Paul Junger Witt, Tony Thomas, and Harris served as the original executive producers: https://en.wikipedia.org/wiki/the_Golden_Girls.

Gail Galvan

In Kewanna, Indiana, Charlie had just fed his dogs and outdoor cats before heading out to the backyard to feed his pot-bellied pig, Lucy. Being a kind of *Sanford and Son* type of country guy, always buying and selling to folks in town, he made sure his cell phone was always at hand. When he noticed Lucy lying quietly in the pig pen, he knew she didn't look right and since she wouldn't get up, he climbed in the muddy pen with his knee high rubber boots to take a look, still smoking his cigarette.

After yelling at her and shaking her, sure enough, Lucy perked up, and as he tried to help her stand up, his cell phone slipped and fell right into the mud. Do you know that phone worked even after digging it out of that mess. The story got around and there was a local cell phone distributor in the next town over, so they asked Charlie and Lucy to star in a commercial, you know, to show how reliable and remarkable their phone is. They said only "water resistant" guarantees, but people still bought the phone like crazy because they liked the story so much.

He made close to $5,000 making that commercial. At first the producer wanted to use the *Cable Guy* star, but they said Charlie was the real thing, too, so if he could say his two lines, he could do it. So he did. I helped him celebrate by having pizza over in Winamac one night at Pizza King.

Texting: Smash-Ups, Mishaps, and Laughs

(Fort Lauderdale, Florida) A mother at the beach one day with her two young kids noticed three very strange things. A teenage girl was actually trying to text while playing volleyball. Her teammates, of course, were yelling at her to put down the phone. Before she did, however, the ball bounced right off her head. A family of four, two adults and two twin sons, about age 12, were all sitting by the water in individual lawn chairs and all four of them were staring down at their phones and texting away. And, as leaving that day, in the parking lot, two girls were jumping up and down while texting. They were barefoot and the pavement was pitch black and boiling hot.

(New York) Two FBI agents, Sam and Cody, were in the middle of a drug bust when Sam's cell phone rang. Cody couldn't believe it when Sam answered his phone and told his girlfriend to hang on; he said he was busy. She hears him yell, "Stop, or I'll shoot!" then hears the gunshots.

"Sam, Sam, what's going on? Are you okay?"

"Yeah, I'm fine Dottie. I just had to kill someone who was shooting at me, that's all…Can I call you back?" Sam saw the look of disbelief on his partner's face. Dottie fainted. After no answer, Sam hung up and continued to chase more bad guys.

(Trenton, New Jersey) While shopping at Walmart, two women crashed into each other's shopping carts because both were texting on their phones. The fight was on. The carts tipped over, fruit got smashed up all over the floor, juice cartons got squished and spilled, and both women slipped and fell. All the shoppers went rushing to the scene to witness the big messy fight. Managers got involved and got slugged. One of the ladies ended up with a broken wrist. It took two police officers to get things under control. What a fiasco at Walmart, just because two women had to text and shop at the same time.

Texting: Smash-Ups, Mishaps, and Laughs

(Valparaiso, Indiana) While working her route one day, a local town bus driver had to restrain one of the passengers. Apparently, about ten people on the bus were all texting and talking on their cell phones. It got very loud, one passenger said, and the upset rider jumped up and yelled that everyone had better hand over their cell phones or he would grab them all and throw them out a window. He shouted, "I mean it, give them all up now, or their history...I'm sick of it, all the obsessed texting, all the yack, yack, yack. I can't hear myself think! There is no peace anymore on this bus. Why isn't it a law, no cell phones?" He grabbed another phone and looked toward the driver.

At that point, Misty found a safe place to pull over. She called in for help, then tried to calm the agitated rider. One passenger was resisting and said, "No, heck with you, no way I'm giving you my phone. Get lost!" They started arguing back and forth, and then Misty got in between them.

"Now you really need to settle down, just calm down and sit. No way you can just take people's phones...now, please, please, just sit down and we'll work this out." She touched the man on his shoulder and he swung at her. Well, that was the wrong thing to do to a past local karate champion. The man was down and knocked out in seconds. Everyone on the bus started jumping up and down and cheering the bus driver on.

"I need a drink! They don't pay me enough for this," said the hero for the day as she handed cell phones back to owners and took her driver's seat.

THE MANNING BROTHERS: GOOFY GOLFING GUYS

Peyton asked his younger brother, Eli, if he wanted to play a round of golf with him one day, since a celebrity golf tournament was coming up and Peyton wanted to stay loose. Eli said, "Sure, Bro, but Sunday would be a better day since I'm kind of busy today." Peyton didn't want to wait, though. He was in the mood. So Eli consented, and they headed out to play golf one day instead of football.

Sometimes, fun-loving men that they are, Peyton and Eli would drive separate golf carts, even compete in races on occasion, go up hills, down hills, from the beginning of the golf course to the entire last hole. Of course they had to rent out the golf course when they really wanted to get silly like that.

Well that particular day Eli had a lot on his mind. He was the best man at his friend's upcoming wedding and planning a bachelor party, so he had to stay in touch, which of course meant lots of phone calls. So his cell phone stayed close by at all times.

"C'mon, you overgrown slow-poke old-timer,

catch up!" Eli yelled back toward Peyton as he raced to the third hole.

While Peyton pushed the accelerator on his golf cart to the floor, Eli answered his cell phone.

"Yeah, Stan. No, no, I go it. I'll call the other guys today, promise. Yeah, yeah, yeah, them, too, and Todd's taking care of the girl jumping out of the cake thing. I got it all under control…don't worry about a thing." He reassured the nervous cousin of the groom.

Just then Eli saw Peyton pull up right alongside of him. Eli shouted, "Gotta go!" He tossed his cell phone down on the seat and tried his best to make a hot rod out of a golf cart.

Head to head they drove on, mumbled, grumbled, laughed, shouted, and finally veered into each other just for the heck of it.

Peyton yelled out, "Are you crazy? I just about went over. Jeez Eli, get a grip, it's just some friendly brotherly golf time here. Dad always did say you never played fair."

Again, cell phone. He ignored it and swung right, hoping to knock into Peyton, but it didn't work.

Texting: Smash-Ups, Mishaps, and Laughs

"Oh shoot, hey, big brother, we need to go rent some real bumper cars!"

"I'm game, but first, I'm gonna sack you!" Peyton surprised Eli, slowed way down, and got directly behind him. Then he sped up and purposely made contact three times.

"Cut that out...you're giving me a migraine."

"Okay, okay. Let's get to the next hole, meet ya there." Peyton slowed down and started to go right, but he heard Eli's cell phone music again, that "Whispering Wizard" tune.

"Hey, I told you...no cell phones on our goofy golfing outing little brother. You need to concentrate on our fun here." He laughed. "Besides, I saw you texting a ways back and how you almost ran into that tree...now you're not stupid enough to text and drive on the road, are ya? Please tell me, Eli."

"No, no, never. I signed that pledge with Oprah years ago, but I gotta get this, real quick. Meet ya at the next hole." Eli stopped his cart and talked to another friend—this time—about lining up some designated "chauffeurs." The party plans included some major drinking buddies. Two phone calls and one text later, Eli caught up to Peyton. They both made a couple of great shots and climbed back into their golf carts.

Just then Eli's phone rang again.

"Oh, c'mon, you're not gonna do it, are you, little brother? Give me a break…you're like some obsessive little sister addicted to her cellie. C'mon, Sissy, let's get rollin'."

"Ah, just one more…then I'll put it away."

Peyton sighed, said he'd be moving on, and called Eli, "Sissy," again. He rode on for just a little ways, then looked back and saw Eli texting. Peyton mumbled, "Oh for Pete's sake, now he's texting…I gotta teach him a lesson." Peyton had been waiting for the perfect moment anyway, a point when Eli was distracted and wouldn't know what was coming.

So Peyton rode back toward Eli and got positioned about six feet to the right of him and a little ways behind. As figured, Eli ignored him and just kept texting away. Peyton took five water balloons out of his duffle bag which was on the seat next to him, and started firing away at Eli's back.

Boom! Splash! Bam! One after another.

Texting: Smash-Ups, Mishaps, and Laughs

Eli held his phone way up in the air, turned around and began to curse at his prankster brother. "What the hell? Are you crazy? We haven't done the water balloon thing in three years." He put his phone down on a dry towel, jumped out of the cart and chased his brother down.

They cursed, wrestled, and laughed until their sides ached. Then they climbed back into their carts and golfed the rest of the eighteen holes.

On the car ride home to continue their visit with their parents, Eli asked, "You're coming to Zach's wedding, right?"

"Yeah, sure, why not…..hey, I wonder just how many couples get married on Valentine's Day."

"Yeah, I wonder. By the way, I think Mom has something special waiting for us at home." Eli said.

"Like what? Apple pie? Her lemon-filled cookies?" Peyton licked his lips.

"No, no…she said she taped the *Kitty Bowl*. I haven't seen it yet, have you?"

"No, too busy playing in the Super Bowl, little brother, if ya know what I mean."

"Oh yeah, I forgot, you big hunky, overgrown

superstar….guess that bumper sticker on your car says it all, huh?"

It read: Super Bowl 50, 2016. Broncos vs. Panthers and the winner is: BRONCOS, of course. GO TEAM!

A couple hours later, boisterous laughter filled the Peyton household as the *Kitty Bowl* entertained.

WITHDRAWAL IS THE WORST

For today's self-help group of teen addicts, there were eleven attending. Those in need gathered every Wednesday evening at the church in a room upstairs. The chairperson for the evening was Melissa. After all of the preliminaries, the meeting began.

"Okay, this meeting is now open....and let's start with Belinda."

Belinda, a 14 year old, twirled her blue hair as she spoke. "I can't sleep, I can't eat. I'm nervous all the time and even mean to everybody just because my mom took my damn cell from me. Two more weeks of this, two freakin' weeks. I can't deal." She crossed her arms, frowned and blurted out, "That's it...all I'm saying is this is cruel and unjust punishment. I'm not a cell phone addict. I'm not...but, yeah, I am a teenager and I need my damn phone. Thank you very much MOTHER!" After a long pause, she said, "That's it. I'm done with this lame sharing shit."

In a perky voice, Melissa, the chairperson said, "Okay, then. Good sharing Belinda. How about you, Fran?"

"Nope, too sick to talk. I mean it. I missed soooo much today, just because I'm doomed to live without a cell phone…until I'm 18 that is, anyway. I even missed an invitation to the prom today by Vance, the dude I wanted to go with. This is ludicrous, just plain cruel, indecent, and injustice at its worst." Fran pushed herself away from the table and sank down in her chair.

"Well, my name is Darielle, and I'm admitting it 'cause I wanna get better. I'm a cell phone addict and it's caused me a lot of grief. I can't say for everybody, but for me, it's like a disease and it kept getting worse and worse and I couldn't stop." She took a sip of water. "It got so bad I got carpal tunnel. I don't know if I will text again, I really don't…just 'cause, I'm not certain I got any control over it. It's like I get possessed, really, you guys, it's sick, and I don't wanna be sick anymore." She took two more sips of water and continued. "Thing is, it seems like an all or nothing thing and I can't handle that. I've tried moderation, honest, tons of times. It does not work for me. So I'm screwed, I guess—a hopeless cell phone addict. Jeez, we got our druggies and alcoholics out there in the world and I get stuck with this stupid, pathetic addiction. I'm screwed…and the withdrawal…oh my God. Been through it many times. It sucks." Darielle let out a long sigh and turned to the next one in the room sitting next to her.

As others spoke, a few tried their best to offer hope and strength to the rest. Nobody seemed to be in very good spirits or handling their cell phone addiction well. Most had been to see doctors for their withdrawal symptoms interfering with their young lives. Only two of the group continued to see a psychologist.

The Tuesday evening meeting wrapped up. Everyone chimed in as usual.

"God grant me the serenity to accept the things I cannot change, the courage to change the things I can, and the wisdom to know the difference."

On the way home, two of the members caved, stopped at Walmart, bought a couple Trac phones and swore they would not get caught by their mom and dad.

Three other members thought they had it all under pretty good control and texted just three simple texts…but the withdrawal symptoms from not being able to text more throughout the evening were just killing them.

"Withdrawal is the worst!" said Melissa to herself as she texted one last time for the night.

"Withdrawal occurs because your brain works like a spring when it comes to addiction." *

*SOURCE: http://800recoveryhub.com/drug-and-alcohol-withdrawal ("Drug and Alcohol Withdrawal" by Victoria Berman October 23, 2015 in Addiction, Alcohol. Courtesy of Victoria Berman. Thank you!)

OBSESSIVE-COMPULSIVE? WHO ME?

"Courtney, look at that poor cute little boy over there. I've been watching and his stupid mom and dad are totally ignoring him." Kassie pointed to the family sitting in a booth at MacDonald's.

"So…so what. Leave it alone, Kassie."

"It's been like ten minutes. The kid keeps trying to get his mom and dad's attention and they just ignore him. She's texting away and the dad is on some kind of business call I think." She took a bite of her cheeseburger and a couple sips of Pepsi. "So I'm gonna go say something if they keep it up."

"No you're not! It's none of your beeswax. Eat your stupid sandwich. We gotta get going pretty soon, and you're one to talk. What about when I try to get your attention when you're on the phone or texting all the time?" Courtney expected a defensive answer, but instead she was ignored. "You're obsessed with texting…not to mention your other real obsessive compulsive disease. It's getting worse, Kassie. I'm telling you, as a best friend, you need to get help."

Again, her friend just shrugged and blew her off. But at the same time, she took her napkin and wiped her mouth ten times exactly. Then, sure enough, after a few more minutes, Kassie couldn't refrain. She walked right up to the family.

"Excuse me," she looked the parents dead in the eyes. "But your son there, he's been trying to get your attention now for over ten minutes."

The mom looked up and seemed shocked while the dad said, "Hold on a minute," to the person on the phone. To Kassie, he asked calmly, "Is this really any of your business young lady?"

"No, not really…but I'm making it my business, sir." She answered back sarcastically. "Just pay him a little attention, will ya?"

"I suggest that you don't butt into our business and get the hell away from us." He looked at his son. "Are you okay, Son?"

"Yeah, Dad, I'm okay…I just wanted to…."

"Fine, see, he's just fine. Now, get lost." He went right back to his phone call.

Kassie spoke mostly to the mother at this point. "Fine, but just remember, your son's right there beside you. He's not invisible." She stomped back to sit with Courtney.

Courtney stared at her friend in disbelief. Kassie, in the meantime, did her calming ritual—tapped her right knee ten times, then her left.

"Happy now? Erin Brockovich, or whoever the child-neglect advocate of the world might be."

"Yeah, much better, thank you. Courtney, you can't always just sit around and not speak up with injustice going on all around you." Kassie preached.

"Okay, okay. Can you finish your Pepsi so we can get out of here?"

"Yeah, sure." She picked up a napkin and wiped the plastic drink container ten times and finished it. She glanced over again at the little boy. "Look, they're still at it. Unbelievable. Poor kid."

"C'mon, we've got to get to swim practice."

Kassie took one more look over at the family and smiled at the little boy who was watching her. He smiled back. His parents never noticed.

Courtney and Kassie grabbed their backpacks and left.

When Kassie got home that evening, she spent

hours organizing the clothes in her closet and drawers. She also made sure the items in the refrigerator were in alphabetical order.

Her final OCD classic get-ready-for-bed behavior was brushing her teeth for exactly three minutes and brushing her long golden brown hair for exactly 100 strokes.

The strange behaviors continued after she climbed into bed and began to text Courtney and a couple of other friends. Before every single text, she had to hit the letters for the saying, it will be ok (i-t-w-i-l-l-b-e-o-k). That way, in case she ever got another devastating text message in her life, it gave her hope that, with the passing of time, things would be okay again.

That's when all of the nonsensical, sickly obsessive-compulsive behaviors began. Kassie's mom blamed herself, of course, but it was the only way she could get a hold of her daughter that day. Kassie had put her cell phone on silence for a class and forgot to put it back on beep. So as a last resort, Mrs. Piper finally decided to text the message: *Please honey, come home right away…your dad is dying. He's taken*

Texting: Smash-Ups, Mishaps, and Laughs

a turn for the worst.

On hospice care for the last 6 months, Mr. Piper was under care at home for his terminal lung cancer. By the time Kassie got home that day, her dad was already gone. So, to her, that meant that her dad probably figured she didn't care enough to stop whatever she was doing and come home. She didn't love him enough to show up, to share one last kiss, one final goodbye.

That's when the apprehension about answering text messages without first performing her safety/reassuring ritual set in.

Three different professionals did their best: a psychiatrist, psychologist, and school counselor, but to no avail. Kassie was definitely getting worse. Until she encountered a close call one day when she was hanging out with Courtney.

They were coming back from the movies one weekend afternoon. As the proceeded down the two lane exit ramp off the highway, they both noticed a female driver to their left who was talking on her cell phone. Of course Kassie wanted to jump out of the car and strangle the woman. At least Kassie always abided by that rule, no calling or texting while driving. She always said that it was just insane to try and do both at the same time.

Courtney sped up a little and tried to get to the stop sign before the lady so she could get away from her, but right at the same time, the other driver sped up, too. Courtney figures the lady must not have seen them since she was busy on the phone because she swerved right into them. On instinct, Courtney veered off further to the right and slammed on the brakes to avoid a collision.

They were okay, but the seconds of terror and screaming really frightened them. After thanking God that they were okay, Courtney got brave and headed home.

Just a few miles up the road, they saw the lady's car all smashed up and knew that she was dead. Her car was squashed like a bug up against a tree off the road. Witnesses at the tragic car wreck scene told officers that they saw her on the phone at the stop sign at the end of the exit ramp, and moments later she just swerved right and crashed into the tree.

That day, like others, hit Kassie hard. She

realized she didn't want to be distracted, or waste precious time doing idiotic unnecessary things—because she said, "It could all end tomorrow. Just like Dad, just like that lady, just like, I don't know, anybody." All of a sudden, plenty of Zen-like philosophical books about living in the present and self-help books about kicking OCD cluttered up her bedroom. She improved quickly, graduated with a 3.7 point average, went on to college, grad school, and so on.

Years later, as a licensed psychologist, Kassie sat across from a 15 year old girl named Marcella. Dr. Piper had to ask her teen client to put her cell phone away three times before she conceded.

After placing the cell phone in her pocket, Kassie noticed the girl open and close both fists over and over again while counting each time.

Dr. Piper asked, "Just a couple simple questions, Marcella…aren't you tired? Wouldn't you like to simplify your life by getting a grip on your addictive and repetitive behaviors?" She smiled the most compassionate smile that she could.

The girl snapped, "Who, me? No. Don't lay

that on me. I'm not a crazy OCD nut. I'm just a normal, everyday teenager who likes her phone." She fidgeted and twirled her blond shoulder length hair.

"Right, sure. Well, let's start there; what's normal? I'd sure like to know because I certainly don't understand that concept. All I know is there is some kind of continuum, like a lifeline that stretches from here to here." She held out her arms as wide as she could. "And somewhere, all along that continuum lies our normal and abnormal behaviors, and some of those repetitive, addictive ones sure make us tired sometimes. Can we agree on that?" Dr. Piper leaned forward with her elbows on her desk.

After a long pause Marcella said, "Yeah, sure. I guess I can cop to that, but I ain't no sick freak; I'm just a teenager living out my life. That's all. Can we agree on that, Doc?"

"Certainly, Marcella. Sure thing. Sounds good to me, a starting point, and I promise you this. I never ever forgot or will forget what it was like to be a teenager or just how incredibly hard it was. I promise…okay?" She held out her hand and Marcella met her half way. They shook on it.

Texting: Smash-Ups, Mishaps, and Laughs

The therapy and healing had begun. Marcella smiled and seemed at ease for a change. She pointed to her T-shirt and asked, "Hey, Doc Piper, you like my shirt? Ya see, I'm gonna major in psychology in college, too."

"Great, Marcella, I look forward to you joining the profession someday then."

ALL BRUISED UP

"Fifth grade is tough, Mom. There's lots of reading—science and math are getting harder. I don't even like my teacher this year, Mrs. Blemmer. Everybody calls her Mrs. Blemish because she's got marks all over her face. Any way I can get you to homeschool me?" Kaylee's voice begged.

"Nope. I've got to work to help pay the bills, sweety. I'm afraid you'll just have to tough it out. But maybe tonight your dad or I can help you with your homework. Now why don't you finish your Corn Flakes and run off to school." Mrs. Conley smiled and gave her 10 year old daughter a quick hug around her shoulders.

"But, Mom!"

"Kaylee, stop it now. You're just being silly. You'll live. I promise. By the way, did you fall or something, again? I see that bruise on your left arm."

"Yeah, I just tripped over my shoes in my room."

"Well, put your shoes up, Kaylee, out of the way, okay? Oh, and don't forget, cell phone is mostly for family." She grabbed her keys off the kitchen counter. "I've got to go, honey, see you tonight. Don't miss your bus."

"Okay, Mom, love you."

"Love you too, sweety."

Five minutes later Kaylee was out the door headed for the bus stop. She hated the heavy backpack and she had a lot on her mind—choir practice, swimming at the Y.M.C.A., and of course homework. But all that didn't keep her from spending time texting her BFFs. She was glad her mom trusted her so far, but it was hard to believe.

With her head down, Kaylee texted away to Muriel, who she had to sing a duet with at a church recital. Then there was Tonya, she just wanted to know if she was still in love with Kip, the cool sixth grader in Mr. Gordon's class.

All of a sudden, bam! She hit the ground. Some kid had left a ball on the sidewalk in front of a house. Kaylee had blue jeans on and luckily there were no tears at the knees, but it sure hurt, and she knew they would be scraped up.

Oh shoot, stupid kids, why in the heck don't kids pick

Texting: Smash-Ups, Mishaps, and Laughs

up after themselves like their parents probably tell them to?

She rubbed her right knee as she got to her feet. Her backpack had slipped off and she had to put the darn heavy thing back on. Finally she came to the bus stop.

"Barbi, I was just gonna text you. You got my blue sweatshirt you borrowed?" Kaylee asked as several kids got on the bus.

"Yeah, I got it. I'll bring it over tonight. Promise. Wanna sit with me today, Kaylee?"

"Yeah. But I gotta text Gloria. You know her mom is in the hospital having another baby?"

"Really? Gosh, that means Gloria will have five kids in her family. Wish I had a brother or sister," Barbi shared.

"No you don't. Trust me. Especially brothers, they're a pain." They both laughed, then Kaylee and Barbi both got busy texting again. After all, they had to take care of a lot of personal business before school started.

Kaylee decided to walk home with Barbi that day to get her sweatshirt instead of waiting on her friend to bring it to her. After leaving Barbi's she was at it again—walking along with a lot on her mind, and got busy texting. Bam!

"Oh no," she whined out loud, "now I'm gonna have another bruise I bet."

She looked down and saw that she had tripped on a crooked sidewalk she knew was there. She had promised herself she would watch out for it.

"I'm gonna sue somebody. Sue? Is that right? Is that what people do when somebody did something wrong and they have to pay for it…sounds just like a girl's name to me." She talked to herself as she got up, rubbed her knees and walked on. "Guess I better put my cell away. I can hear Mom now."

After supper, Kaylee was getting ready for a swim at the Y when her mom knocked on her bedroom door, and went in to ask her a question.

"Kaylee, I wanted to ask…Oh my God, Kaylee, where did you get all those bruises from? What in the name of heaven, child. Are you okay?" She rushed toward her. "Sit down here, on the bed; let me look at you." Her mom counted at least eight bruises, some still deep purplish in color, others red, some brownish and fading, and the two scraped knees. Mrs. Conley could see those were very new.

"Mom, chill. I'm okay, nothing really hurts. Well, maybe except my knees, they kind of sting a little. I'm not shot and bleeding to death. Jeez."

"I want to know right this minute how you got all these!" She demanded.

"Uh…well, I fell."

"You fell? You fell why, where? How many times?"

"Jeez, Mom. You're acting like the police. I just fell a couple times. Guess my knees or ankles maybe or something just gave out and I fell. It's no big deal." She got up and started to pull her jeans up over her swimsuit.

"Well, I'm taking you to the doctor if you are just falling out of the blue. We'll get some blood tests, and…hey, wait a minute, now I want to make sure; this isn't some kind of bullying thing is it? I know you're my sweet little Kaylee, but you're also a tomboy who has told me in the last week that you hate at least three people at school. You haven't been getting into fights have you? Now tell me the truth."

"No, Mom. No. No. No. I just fell."

"Oh God. Well, kids don't just fall all the time and get lots of bruises for no reason, and certainly you've never done it before."

"We gotta go, Mom, I'll be late."

"Okay, finish dressing, meet me downstairs, but I'm getting you an appointment with Dr. Pesky."

"Okay, Mom."

As soon as her mom left the room Kaylee started brainstorming how to get herself out of the mess she had just gotten herself into. No way she could tell her it's all the cell phone's fault…and people she had every right to sue. Every fall was related to texting. *What the heck am I going to do? Good one, Kaylee.*

Turns out, Kaylee didn't have to make that doctor's appointment. Her mom decided to follow Kaylee home from school one day. She knew she had to stay after school for choir practice, so she'd be walking home. Mrs. Conley borrowed her brother's car and stayed back a ways, so she could make sure Kaylee wouldn't notice her mom playing detective. She didn't want to see her daughter fall down and fathom that some bone or muscle disease, or worse, had stricken her. But, she kind of wished she would fall, so she could see it for herself. And sure enough, three blocks from home, Kaylee went down. Not only that, she fell in the street. No cars were coming, thank God, and the mystery got solved, thank God.

Mrs. Conley couldn't believe it. She was so disappointed in Kaylee. After all the safety talks about everything. There was a small raised bumpy area in the street and because Kaylee was texting, she didn't see it, and bam! Her mom couldn't believe it. She actually witnessed it. Yeah, Kaylee looked both ways before she started to cross the street, but then she looked down and started texting. That's when Mrs. Conley saw her trip and fall. Well, obviously, her mom drove up a little closer, parked on the side of the street and went to help Kaylee. It all had to be discussed out in the open now, anyway, how she just happened to be there. That's when Mrs. Conley saw the bumpy street pavement.

"Mom, what the heck are you doing here?"

"Helping you out of the street, my dear daughter. Well, I see nobody is bullying you, and I also saw you walking down the sidewalk texting away and then texting again as you were in the middle of the street. What in the world...?"

"I know, Mom. I know. I'm all bruised up. It hurts. I'm tired of it. Here, you can have my stupid phone for a while. My friends can call me at home." She handed her mom the cell phone as if it had caused all of her troubles. "Stupid cell phone....Hey, wait a minute. What are you doing here? Where's our car?"

As they both climbed into Mrs. Conley's brother's car, she explained her decision to play detective.

"Oh, Mom, you watch too much *Murder, She Wrote*."

"Well, that might be true, but you, my dear, don't watch where you are going. So yes, I will take your phone...for two weeks, and you can have it back when I am certain this is not going to happen again. Do you understand?" She looked over at Kaylee.

"Yes, Mom. Hey, can we have pizza tonight?"

SOCIOLOGICALLY SPEAKING

Marleen and Marie, two energetic Denver college students, had their weekend all planned out. First they'd take Marleen's sisters and their kids to the Elitch Gardens Theme Park since they'd never been there before. And on Sunday, they couldn't wait for all of them to ride up to Echo Lake. On Sunday, Marleen couldn't keep bragging about how she had been to the top of Mount Evans once and how magnificent the vista point was, "It was like standing on a cloud looking out into heaven."

After their Rocky Mountain High weekend, it was back to classes. Marleen had to get everything ready so that Marie could help her with her sociology assignment on Tuesday. They planned to spend the whole day on the Auraria Campus, collecting data (of sorts) with regard to students and their cell phones.

Marie really wanted that A, so she intended to make her sociological observation paper an interesting one. Marleen agreed to help her observe students, ask questions, write down stuff, and report back to Marie.

Cell phones, and students' obsession with them—Professor Rhodes, at Metropolitan State University, thought it was a great idea and said the topic served as a modern day, social media, valuable connection theme. Of course, Dr. Rhodes was only filling in for a temporarily absent teacher, he actually taught philosophy, but Marie was enjoying him. She couldn't wait to take his philosophy class the next semester.

The first part of Tuesday morning went by fast; both students bothered other fellow students and were surprised how many would take a few minutes away from their cell phones or walking to class to answer questions. But there were those who said, "No way, I'm on my way to class," or some who just kept talking or texting.

The two students playing reporters, or sociological detectives as they liked to refer to themselves, walked all around outside, spent some time near the library, waited outside of classes, hung around the bookstore, and then met at the Tivoli Student Food Court for lunch.

"Hey, let's eat at Dazbogs again, they've got

that great Russian coffee." Marie suggested.

"Nah, we went there last time. It's my turn. Let's go to Alfresco's for the turkey wrap. Please?" Marleen whined in a high-pitched voice.

"Oh all right. Hey, do you know what Dazbog means? I do, it means 'cheers.' So I guess if we're drinking our coffee there, we're supposed to click cups and say, 'cheers.'"

"Well, that's not what I heard. I think it's some major God-dude in Slavic mythology, you know, like a hero."

"Well that's not what the waitress told me," Marie insisted.

"So we'll look it up later, just see who is right." Marleen said.

"Okay, okay, but, hey, you got a lot of good stuff for me?" Marie asked enthusiastically.

"Oh yeah, and you?"

"Oh yeah, God it was sad, Marleen, this one girl, I couldn't believe she could even talk to me about it. She had two friends, one was driving and texting and she crashed into her best friend on the road. This friend of hers had actually killed her best friend all because of texting…so sad."

"Oh man, Marie, tragic, just like we saw on the videos, huh?" The waitress interrupted and they both ordered a turkey wrap and Chamomile tea. "Let's see, at first, like you were looking for, I didn't see anybody bumping into each other, but sure enough about the second hour it started. So all in all, I've got four people yacking on cell phones that bumped into someone else because they were not paying attention."

"Really, oh cool…me too, I got a few."

"Yeah, Marie, these two girls actually almost got into a fight because the one walked straight into the other and both of their phones went down. They were just about to fight but when they figured out both phones still worked the one just shoved the other and told her to 'watch it.'" Marleen flipped her jet black hair off of her shoulders.

"Oh man, thanks, good stuff detective. I got some great data, too. I'll put it all together tonight and show you tomorrow, okay?"

"Sure, Marie, but we're going out again, right? I still haven't asked a lot of the questions you wanted me to." Marleen took a sip of her tea.

"Yeah, oh yeah. Thanks for sticking it out. Don't forget the implant question—If it wouldn't hurt anything, ever, health-wise or environmentally, would the person be willing to put an implant invention in his/her ear so they never had to carry a cell phone again?"

"I know, I know, it's the final question on the questionnaire, right?"

Marie confirmed and as she finished her lunch, she brushed her long golden brown hair and replenished her red lipstick. "I got three people who fell, couldn't believe it. I was afraid of that, too, that I wouldn't get anybody to admit that. Okay, so you ready, partner?"

"Ready, but first you said you'd tell me about Shane, how is the lust going?" Marleen laughed.

"You mean, love….we're in love Marleen, love, L-O-V-E, love." Her friend emphasized.

"Yeah, right. You mean lust. We'll see if this romance lasts more than three months. Let's go get your data."

They both smiled at each other and went about

their sociological business.

That night as Marie sat in her room, she put together all the data and constructed her paper. She still lived at home since her mom and dad insisted on saving her rent money. She was a bit compulsive once she started on something. Sure, she could take a few days, but once she started something, until it was done, it played on her mind. Curiosity played a role, too, she couldn't wait to see what her "subjects" had said.

Luckily, it wasn't an assignment for statistic's class. She knew that was going to be so much more grueling and have to be more precise with information and numbers. But Dr. Rhodes had made it clear, general information and sociological insight was mainly what students were supposed to report back about for this particular research study.

Marleen and Marie both collected numbers for how many cell phone users did this and that as well as some interesting comments regarding the "practically can't live without" the modern day invention.

"I'd die if I didn't have my cell phone, I'd just die," said many of the responding students.

Texting: Smash-Ups, Mishaps, and Laughs

Do they really think they'd die without their phones? Sure....that's just crazy lame stupid. Modern day "kids," Marie thought to herself, *they don't know just how easy they have it. After all, there was a time when phones didn't exist at all—or electricity for that matter.*

And, with the exception of nine subjects, all the rest said yes to the idea that they would let someone put something in their head, surgically, some kind of implant, if it meant a cell phone of some sort could be installed! (Without any repercussions, as stated.) She couldn't believe it.

The next day, Marie shared her paper, and all the numbers and yesses and no's, and comments with Marleen. Marleen said she knew for sure that Marie had aced it, the paper deserved an A+ as far as she was concerned. Here were some of the questions:

1. How many students and people going by appeared to have cell phones? How many did not?

2. How many were using them? How many were not using them?

3. If on cell phones, were they paying attention to where they were going?

4. Did any bump into others or objects?

5. Did any subjects fall?

6. When approached, was subject annoyed or did he/she take time to answer questions?

7. Did subject ever talk on phone and drive?

8. Did subject ever text and drive?

9. Did subject ever make a pledge to NOT talk on phone and/or text and drive?

10. Did subject know anybody who was hurt or killed which was related to texting and driving?

11. Would subject watch a video on tragic accidents about texting and driving? And do they think it would make a difference?

12. If a cell phone could be implanted into subject's head, without any health-wise or environmental adverse effects, and it would allow their hands to be completely free, would subject agree to do it?

13. Do you feel like a text addict sometimes?

"Good popcorn, Marie. You got some more caffeine free Pepsi?" Marleen requested as she sat on a bean bag in Marie's bedroom finishing up reading her paper. "This is good stuff, Marie, really, I just know you aced it...*AND I HELPED!*"

"Yep, you sure did. Here, I'll get you some

Texting: Smash-Ups, Mishaps, and Laughs

more pop, then you wanna watch *Ascending Jupiter*?" She grabbed Marleen's glass.

"Sure...sounds good."

"Oh, and by the way, Shane and I broke up. He's boring...time to move on."

Both girls laughed and Marleen couldn't help giving her BFF an "I told you so" look.

"Yeah, yeah, yeah," Marie snapped back. "You think you know everything. I'll find true, everlasting love someday my friend, and so will you. Hey, you left your Field Interviewer I.D. in my car. Here it is, save it, a college souvenir to remember the good 'ol days. Let me get you that pop, then we'll watch the movie...or, I actually have some wine."

"Now you're talking. Let's chill."

Best Friends Forever...Field Interviewers for a day

"WE DREAM ON TWO WHEELS!"

KATE'S

CHERYL'S

CAN'T KILL A DREAMER ON TWO WHEELS

Some stories share happy endings, some sad endings. Then there are the stories that include the good news, bad news elements, both happy endings and sad events. This is one of those.

One sunny day in Cannon Beach, Oregon, an amazingly healthy seventy year old woman and her forty year old daughter took one last breathtaking look at the Pacific Ocean. They finished up packing; then they set sail for their remarkable adventure, but not on a boat.

No, Cheryl and her mom dreamed on two wheels, and they always rode on two wheels, whether it was an incredible cross-country bicycle tour or a "more simple" trek of say, 700 or a 1,000 miles.

This trip they intended to ride from Cannon Beach, Oregon to cross the Golden Gate Bridge in San Francisco. Cheryl often envisioned crossing over the bridge with her mom on their bikes. She couldn't wait to get started, live out another dream, and create more unforgettable memories.

"Mom…Mom, you ready?" Cheryl tied her hair back into a ponytail and smiled.

"Ready, honey. Let's hit the road. Just let me take one last sip of water before we head out." She grabbed her water bottle from the bike water holder.

"Okay, Mom." She started walking back toward the hostel where they had stayed the night. They enjoyed talking to Ron, a bicyclist who had traveled four thousand miles. Of course, they had asked him a hundred questions about his adventure so far. He lived in Canada and was headed north.

Shortly after saying their goodbyes to the friendly hostel staff and Ron—the two bicycle-touring adventurers were on their way, heading south toward San Francisco, California on Highway 101.

The bike shop in town had furnished a few last minute equipment needs the evening before, so they were all set. The weather was exceptional—clear, hot, and dry, which set the mood. They had known about rainy days in California and it was the one thing that caused the most worry for some reason. Cheryl and her mom, like most bicyclists, cherished nice, accommodating weather.

Texting: Smash-Ups, Mishaps, and Laughs

Twenty miles down the road, a couple decided to travel with Cheryl and her mom, Kate, until they all reached Cape Meares for the night.

The next day, their touring companions headed for Cape Lookout while Cheryl and Kate stayed closer to Highway 101. Toward dusk they had reached their destination for the night.

"Hi, excuse me, could you tell me if you have a hostel in town or if your motel is very expensive?" Cheryl asked a female policeman while becoming infatuated with the flickering lights on the dispatcher's switchboard.

"No, I'm afraid Washington City doesn't have a hostel. I don't know how much they charge over there, Hank, do you have any idea what Wilson charges for the night?" She answered the phone and started giving someone directions.

They noticed the big fat cigar the male officer was smoking. "Well, I'll tell ya, I'd say it'd run you about twenty dollars over there at Wilson's place. You're traveling all by yourself, where are you two gals from?"

"We're from Portland. We rode yesterday with

some people but they wanted to go in closer toward Cape Lookout, someone told me it was real hilly, that it'd be easier sticking to 101, so we did. We wanted to make a little time today. I'm Cheryl and this is my mom, Kate."

"On a bicycle, huh? Wow. You want some coffee?" the officer asked. "And just how far are you going?"

"No, no, thanks, we don't drink coffee; can I try some of your water from your fountain?" Switching her helmet from her right hand to the left, Cheryl walked towards the water fountain and took a Dixie cup from the wall and started filling it. Turning her head, she told them both about the San Francisco destination plan, then asked how long they had worked at the jail.

"Oh, I've been here about ten years now. Amber, you've been here what, seven?"

"Yeah, I guess, eight actually, I think." Cheryl and Kate kept asking them questions, they continued to make inquiries, and the four of them kept giving answers. Needless to say, as usual, the adventurous bikers always amazed everyone that they came in con-

Texting: Smash-Ups, Mishaps, and Laughs

tact with.

As the mileage continued to accumulate the next day, the road flattened out except for a very tough climb through the Siuslaw National Forest. A walk for a short distance helped for regaining strength. The main fears that haunted the two now were log trucks, unleashed dogs, and reaching a place to stay before darkness. Julian, a bicyclist from France, came pedaling along and they rode with him for a while. He averaged about one hundred miles in one day, and even though Cheryl and Kate had managed that feat a few times, for this ride, they wanted to take their time and planned to ride about 40 to 60 miles a day.

Friday, they spent the night at a biker's camp, Jesse Honeymoon State Park, a bike and hike, and it cost fifty cents.

"Mom, I'll set up the tent, you just relax, okay?"

"Sure, sweety, thanks." Kate sat down and began to rub her Achilles' tendons. Early in the day, she had to ride standing up at times and used the center of her feet so that the pain eased somewhat. Hot showers sounded terrific, but that evening Cheryl had to deliver the bad news.

"Sorry, Mom, but that shower water is barely a tepid temperature, it is not gonna sooth our achy muscles and tendons very much, I'm afraid. Maybe the next stop…but it feels good to be clean again, not grubby and sweaty. Really, Mom, the water was barely warm." Kate sighed but accepted it.

Serene late evening moments were among the mom and daughter's favorite times.

"Another beautiful day, no rain as of yet, the weather has been so kind. I'm lovin' it, Mom, what about you?" She bit into some celery and sipped on a (no sugar added) cup of apple juice.

"Loving every minute of it, sweety, and our time together, of course." Kate bit into a ripe peach. "Just look at that moon—it's absolutely gorgeous!"

"Yeah, it's so bright and huge tonight…how are the Achilles?"

"Better with rest, that's for sure."

The next day, they traveled from Honeymoon State Park to Coos Bay where Kate experienced a blowout on the back inner tube, which took about fifteen minutes to fix. From there, they pedaled on to

Texting: Smash-Ups, Mishaps, and Laughs

Port Orford. The Port Orford Motel was about sixty miles from the California border. Cheryl rang the bell at the front desk and a lady shouted from a back room that she would be right with her. The owner was so concerned that the two of them were traveling alone. She explained that there had been some trouble in the area with single girls, murders, one they had found, the other one they hadn't.

That was a long night! For the first time, they actually thought about calling it quits and giving up. They wanted a challenge, but plans certainly included returning home eventually, in one piece. Visions of crossing the Golden Gate Bridge became clear that night as they closed their eyes, though, and after a fairly short discussion, they decided to continue.

After all, they'd been on the road many days and nights, together, and never had any real dangerous situations occur. But they knew they had to be very cautious and keep an eye out for other bicyclists to tour with. On Monday all of the work was left up to bicyclists since the tailwind had disappeared and the climbs were outrageous. Although a relaxed, inner pea peaceful feeling became more pronounced as the long days of pedaling eventually got easier.

Following Port Orford, only two other events aroused fear, experiences which left Cheryl and Kate with apprehensive thoughts and a degree of soul-searching as to why they continued to take touring trips which might put themselves in harm's way.

On one occasion, a rather large man driving a plain white milk truck without any printing on the sides of it stopped at the same rest area as they did. The man struck up a conversation. Both tried to remain calm, but daylight was slipping away, and there was just something about him they didn't like.

Not many people were around because tourists were driving up, taking a quick look from the vista view, then leaving. Pedaling away, Cheryl and Kate made sure they were on the lookout. A little further up the road, they saw it, the same white truck, parked barely off to the side. There was no way in the world that they were passing by it. Kate motioned back at Cheryl to stop for a minute. Then, impetuously, Kate waved at the next oncoming car and after seeing it was a woman and two kids in a handy truck, asked if she would drive the two of them

Texting: Smash-Ups, Mishaps, and Laughs

to the campground just down the road. They threw the bikes into the back of the truck and hopped in.

Another time almost left Cheryl with one leg to ride home with. It happened off on a mountainous, country road. While working her way up a steep hill one day near a few scattered houses, her sights had been preoccupied with a couple of dogs to the left when suddenly a mean-looking dog from the right lunged toward her—growling, showing his teeth, and proceeding to attack the first body part the out of control animal could get a hold of. She performed the obvious instinctive response and immediately screamed. Luckily, the dog reacted to her scream like a coward and backed off, whimpering as he left.

The coastline terrain got tougher as they rode along with two German girls, a man and a woman from Florida, and a friendly Australian on a tandem. A few of them knew the territory and explained that they could all look forward to a difficult welcoming California climb tomorrow. The park's biker-hiker area hosted a full house that night. All the cyclists set up their tents, but didn't turn in before relaxing. They all gathered around a mesmerizing campfire, shared great stories, enjoyed their amazing company, and marveled at the sparkling stars and full moon.

Cheryl and Kate felt safe and terrific. Parts of their bodies ached but it was a good feeling, like being tired after a long, hard day's work. They went to sleep knowing that they'd be in California by the next day.

They awoke to the brightest sunshine, began to study the list of parks and bike and hike camps and looked over some other information regarding hostels in San Francisco. Also, within Cheryl's baggage somewhere, which hung in panniers attached to the bike rack on a back wheel, was a hospitality directory. It consisted of a list of names and addresses started by a bicyclist in California. Bicycling tourists could put their names on the list and make contacts with fellow bikers and spend the night in a home rather than a motel. The directory hadn't offered any practical possibilities in Oregon.

Everyone left at different times that morning. Cheryl and Kate left the earliest. Once they woke up, that was it; the adventurers were always ready to travel.

The following night Cheryl was busy and could

Texting: Smash-Ups, Mishaps, and Laughs

not write much in her journal. Instead, the evening was spent sipping wine, and eating homemade biscuits which had been cooked over an open fire. As Kate attempted to bravely walk by three large, horned, beautiful Roosevelt Elk, but froze, a charming middle-aged couple motioned for her to walk through their campsite, and then invited the two of them to dinner. Cheryl explained that a peanut butter sandwich and some fruit were on the menu for the evening, but when they insisted, their kind invitation was accepted without further resistance. Cheryl didn't eat the stew, though, and explained why. She had gone the vegetarian route years ago.

Tackling the Redwoods with their own two legs was a good day's work. They had traveled from Harris Beach (Brookings) to Prairie Creek Redwoods Park, approximately sixty miles. A chilly, damp night made then wish (briefly) that they were back home in a warm bed, but the sweet couple and the glittering campfire managed to make things more comfortable. As Kate walked, she used the centers of her feet rather than flexing toes that evening because her ankles were making a strange, squishing noise. She assumed that fluid had accumulated due to inflammation. But she didn't care, because at last, they were in California.

In the morning Cheryl telephoned and reached a person from the hospitality directory. A male voice answered although a Josie J. Foster had been the name listed. They talked for a minute about the trip. He (Glen) sounded genuinely concerned when Cheryl explained about her mom's painful ankle development. Glen offered to let the bicycling travelers stay for a night or two, or as long as necessary. Cheryl wondered where the girl named Josie was, but didn't ask any questions at the time.

They arrived, finally, but not without some truly agonizing pain, and settled into their first bicycling hospitality host's apartment. Glen attended Humboldt State University in Arcata and majored in psychology. Blonde, tall, and gorgeously handsome were a few things that Cheryl noticed about him as they all introduced themselves. He had to run off to class, so he told Cheryl and Kate to make themselves at home.

"Can you believe this, Mom? He just acts like:

Texting: Smash-Ups, Mishaps, and Laughs

"Here, make yourself at home." Maybe we're like a Bonnie and Clyde or something or Thelma and Louise just posing as cyclists so we can get into places and rip off people...amazing, the trust by some people." She flopped down on the flower-patterned couch. "Man, this is the life. Let's just tour forever, Mom, never go home."

"Oh my, now you're getting a little too obsessive. Think we better keep our lives going, too. What do you say—just bicycle vacations my dear daughter?" She sat down in a recliner chair and started to rub her ankles.

"Here, Mom, you better get your shoes and socks off...I'll get the ice pack." Cheryl jumped up.

"Okay, I'm going to the bathroom first, though. And I think we should clean up a bit before lounging around on this furniture anymore, don't you?"

"Yeah, sure, I guess."

After washing up, (they planned to ask if they could actually shower later, when their host returned), in the living room, all stretched out and snacking and drinking fluids to replenish, Cheryl came across a paper Glen had written about discovering the real self, struggling for the Jungian self and living a life of choices instead of merely existing and building up defenses. The paper went on to describe how some people try to climb the mountain to the top and that's what counts, the steps along the way and being willing to go for it—although once you got there, you discovered that it was only the beginning. The top of one mountain is just the bottom of another one looming ahead. And, that sometimes, consequently, there seemed to be a futility about our efforts and life.

I found out later that it reflected John Dewey's commentary in Glen's own words. The paper inspired Cheryl, not only that, but she identified with it because there she was…right in the midst of everything that the paper suggested. Her mom and her were climbing mountains, real ones *and* philosophically. They had it "made" for a couple of days. It turned out that Glen was single, although he had been married once, and Josie and he were simply sharing the expenses of the apartment. He explained that she was actually the bicycle enthusiast and off on vacation somewhere. Cheryl and Kate both said they were certainly sorry they missed her.

Texting: Smash-Ups, Mishaps, and Laughs

Arcata—with its college atmosphere, parks and unique historical and cultural shops on Main Street—was a sight. Cheryl and Kate accepted where the circumstances had led them and needed a good rest, so they decided to stay for a few days. Actually, it would have been very difficult to turn down the opportunity or the company that they were thoroughly enjoying.

A hot tub of water that evening, leisurely soaking and relaxing, relieved some of the disturbing pain in Kate's ankles, but she could tell the situation was serious at this point. Besides that agony, a lip full of oncoming cold sores began to annoy Cheryl. *Right in front of a hunk, I get stuck with these ugly lips*, she thought. She took out some Anbesol and applied it to try and keep the swelling down to a minimum. After the Anbesol, she spread some Vitamin E oil all over them to assist in boosting her confidence that they would soon begin to disappear. Both Cheryl and Kate enjoyed an unbelievably comfortable, restful night.

For the next several days, moments of great beauty and serenity crept into their lives. Sometimes they'd walk around exploring Arcata, often they simply sat in the park and relaxed while Kate dog and bird-watched and Cheryl wrote in her journal.

In the apartment, while Glen was away at college on his way to becoming a psychologist, a cat named Bugs, a dog named Pam, and some young neighbors from upstairs kept things exciting. Philosophical discussions, movies, and popcorn at night were a lot of fun, too. Kate's ankles were really enjoying the reprieve and healing because of the well-needed rest along with her daily Aleve.

On the fourth day, they knew it was time to leave. The tourists were more determined than ever to complete the trip and reach, at least, one more of their ambitious "mountaintops." The last night they spent in Arcata was delightful. Cheryl and Kate said their goodbyes as they left bright and early the next morning, pedaling down the hill, waving.

Richardson Grove was the stop for the following night, about eighty miles from Arcata. The next day the first twenty-five miles were accomplished at a slow pace. It was referred to as a day when the road cheats. It constantly puts climbs before you, but seemingly doesn't make up for it with downhill rides.

Texting: Smash-Ups, Mishaps, and Laughs

The sun shone intensely. The heat felt as if it melted into the cyclists' bodies, and turned exposed parts bright red, even with suntan lotion applied.

Little things annoyed Cheryl that day. Her ugly lips still hurt, a squeak developed, and of all things, two spokes busted. Although she carried tools and a bicycle repair book, she wasn't really prepared for all emergencies. The practical and mechanical aspects about bicycle trips became even more important to Cheryl after reading *Zen and the Art of Motorcycle Maintenance*. She knew she had to keep her bicycle maintained and know how to fix things—as much as she could. But it seemed, occasionally something would pop up and stump her for a bit.

Being prepared and an analytical thinker, not to mention perseverant as hell, she just assumed that if anything came up, she'd figure out something. Or maybe, even, it would be her mom that would figure it out and solve a certain dilemma.

Unfortunately, something came up and no bike shops were around along that strip of the highway. She pulled up to a vista point to think for a while. She didn't really even know if the instance of broken spokes was a serious matter or not. A few bikers traveled by and waved. Then three male bicyclists stopped and they started talking. She couldn't believe it, one of them carried along extra spokes. She just couldn't believe it. The potential problem, serious or not, was solved by a kind donation.

Again, with the luck. Their bodies and minds rested that evening while spending the night with an extremely interesting family in Ukiah. Steve, a member of a bike club, had his name on the hospitality registry. The family consisted of: mother, father, brother and sister. Steve and his sister seemed to compete against each other for some reason.

For supper everyone enjoyed mashed potatoes, porcupine meatballs, Brussel sprouts, and ice cream. Steve, a young-looking twenty-three-year-old, loved the outdoors and bicycle touring. His mom and dad explained an interesting habit Steve had; he hardly ever slept indoors at night. Only one other tourist had stopped by their house, Cheryl and Kate were the second and third ones, after three years.

Steve was so helpful in the morning, almost overloading Cheryl with information, as he explained about the upcoming road's characteristics in detail. He examined both bikes, and sprayed WD-oil liberally over any potentially squeaky areas. Then he gave Cheryl two maps and pointed out the best way to San Francisco. It was a good thing, too, because on the highway, after a short distance, bicycles were no longer allowed, and a frontage road had to be used instead.

There's only one way to describe Steve—profoundly amazing. If people thought Cheryl and Kate were crazy, off on a bike trip, they certainly would have been impressed if they heard how many miles Steve had toured. One trip extended from the West Coast to the East Coast, a total of seven thousand miles in two months and included some torturing heat while pedaling through the Death Valley Desert area. A map with thumbtacks marked the route and decorated a wall in the house.

Santa Rosa and an upcoming wine tour were on the near future agenda.

As Cheryl and Kate pedaled away from Glen's the next morning, Cheryl thought to herself, *God I slept good, and what nice people.* Then she started singing.

"San Francisco, open your Golden Gate, open your Golden Gate…" It always felt incredible when finish lines approached and she knew she had accomplished such a challenging physical and mental quest…especially her mom, still going strong, at seventy years old.

The concept of self-imposed limits contributed to much of her thinking as she rode along for the rest of the trip. After all, she had often broken through the barriers of many supposed limitations. Not just a year ago, she could barely get out of bed. The diagnosis was chronic fatigue syndrome. It took months and months of fighting back to regain any kind of energy, to get well. Yet, here she was, "back on the road again," and feeling like a million bucks. Well, better than money. Feeling like the luckiest person in the world.

They wound up at a place called the Wayside Nursery that night, Monday, October 1st. Tim, Lucy, and their baby Jimmy were hosts. They owned quite a bit of land, I'm not sure how many acres. The family lived in Tim's homemade abode, although according to him, they were wealthy. They didn't even bother

Texting: Smash-Ups, Mishaps, and Laughs

with electricity. Their personalities were unique. Lucy breastfed Jimmy.

They practiced a different kind of lifestyle, self-sufficiency and simplicity. Their diet consisted mostly of fish and plenty of organic fruits and vegetables. It almost appeared, however, that their revolutionary ideas for change had thrown them into the opposite extreme, one which left Lucy wondering if Jimmy should get his immunization shots or not and also included the use of *un*pasteurized milk. Cheryl was well-educated and worked in the environmental protection field, but she didn't feel like discussing the controversy on the bike trip, so she just let it go.

The cyclists woke up to a "cock-a-doodle-do early the next morning, and hit the road again.

The scenery became more beautiful, with flatter land, country roads, grape vineyards, and Mexican-Spanish-Indian workers everywhere wearing sombrero hats. Temperatures had reached a scorching ninety-five degrees. Experiencing October and summer simultaneously felt strange. They toured the Italian Swiss Wine Colony, and happily sampled some wines. Cheryl pretended to be a connoisseur, and Kate asked a lot of questions. After buying a few postcards, it was time to ride.

By October 2nd, the adventurers had made it. As expected, approaching the finish line left the dreamcatchers feeling like a couple of the luckiest people in the world. After all, not everyone gets to dream big and succeed. Both cyclists knew that.

Cheryl couldn't explain all of her feelings and thoughts when she first saw the majestic Golden Gate Bridge and knew that she was about to cross over her destination after hundreds of miles of good hard, determined work and fun. Actually, she felt too exhausted to jump up and down or anything like that and all of a sudden, as if to spoil the moment, she realized that they still had a long way to go to get back home—not biking it, but making all of the arrangements.

It felt as if she had just realized yet another mountain to climb before the trip could end. Yet, there is no doubt that an amazing sense of joy and completeness accompanied both tourists' feelings, since they had finished what they had set out to do.

Texting: Smash-Ups, Mishaps, and Laughs

But Cheryl, especially, kept thinking to herself, *I've run my marathon, AFTER that chronic fatigue madness—conquered my own pain and fear that I would never be able to ride again.*

Kate, of course, felt really proud of her daughter, and relieved that she was her strong, energetic, healthy self again. And, she knew that this trip, like all of them, was a special accomplishment, again, knowing in her heart, that age is just a number. It should not stop people from fulfilling their dreams.

"Yeah, Mom," Cheryl said after they reached the other side of the Golden Gate, "crossing finish lines is great, but it was all of the traveling along the way, the process which has already taken place, all the wonderful memories with you, my dear, amazing mom, that I'll cherish."

"Ah, me too, sweetheart….now, let's go get something to eat and figure out where we are going to stay tonight. What do you think, a fancy motel for a change? Let's live a little and celebrate." She patted her daughter on the left shoulder and they hugged.

"Sure, Mom, let's celebrate."

Here's that twist, though. Just when a dreamer

thinks he or she has it made, it's all done and over, fine and good, dream accomplished. Bam! The rest of the evening was *not* spent in a restaurant joyously celebrating or in a fancy motel resting up...or planning a long-awaited welcoming trip home.

The way it was told to the police officer by witnesses and Cheryl—it went like this.

"I saw my mom ahead of me, some lady honked. I turned my head to the left and saw her driving and talking on her cell phone. I thought, why is she honking? My mom and I were over to the right side of the road as far as we could be. Just as my mom got to the corner stop sign, she stopped, put her right hand out to signal turning right, then started up again, that's when the lady in the car turned the corner, too, and plowed right into Mom." Cheryl started to break down in tears again. A crowd had gathered and one woman was kind enough to hand her a Kleenex.

"Yeah, I saw the whole thing. That lady was, for sure, talking on her phone, I don't know if she was texting, too, but for sure she had her phone out. I was just walking up to the stop sign and had already

Texting: Smash-Ups, Mishaps, and Laughs

waved to this young lady and her mom as they rode by. Then her mom turned and that lady in the car turned and smashed right into her. I couldn't believe it. I just couldn't believe it, officer."

So that's the bad news, the unhappy part. But, at least, Kate didn't die. Mom and daughter didn't get to celebrate that night in San Francisco. No, that night, and many days and nights after were spent visiting each other in a hospital and rehab center. It was touch and go for a while.

But four months later, after Kate got out of rehab, recovering from many broken bones along with internal injuries, they sure did celebrate then.

The distracted driver, she got fined and probation for a year. Never even took her license. Her insurance had to pay Kate's medical bills, at least.

Two years after that accident, Cheryl and Kate were bicycling across the U.S. with ten other adventure touring cyclists. For some lucky dreamers, the dreams never seem to end. The mountaintops just keep getting more beautiful and meaningful.

One distracted driver, potential dream killer, failed to end the life of one remarkable dreamer on two wheels—but she certainly almost did.

Dream on, Kate and Cheryl, dream on! That's the bumper sticker on Kate's bike. *We dream on two wheels* decorates Cheryl's bike.

How drab and boring life would be, without our dreamers and adventurers to inspire us.

Author's Note: Portions of this story, with revisions, were extracted from *Autobiography of an Allergic/Asthmatic Survivor*, 2014, Gail (Davis) Galvan.

PART THREE:

ON THE CONTEMPLATIVE SIDE

THINK ABOUT IT: Deadly Roadways

Think about it…
How sometimes badness
cancels out goodness.
Sadness triumphs over gladness.
Darkness devours the sunlight.
And with best intentions,
we're scarred by clever inventions.

Think about it…
A pledge to play it safe.
Not mess with chance, disrupt fate.
Then broken promises, deadly turns.
Victims crash and burn,
suffer endlessly, cry and die.
Terminated hellos, gut-wrenching goodbyes.

Think about it…
Seven little letters:
"R U there?"
Texted—with eyes elsewhere.

Not on the road with drivers ahead,
but pushing buttons,
glances, distractions…and then…so dead.

Think about it…
"Damn, I wish, I WISH these drivers
would put down their cell phones.
I'm driving and want to make it home.
I even motion to one man, perform a facial plea.
Phone still in hand—
he simply laughs at me."

Think about it…
Minds tune out
toward descension to attention.
"Sup?"
Three little letters, momentary distractions
and no doubt—again, lives lost
to texting fatal attractions.

Think about it…
The haunting harm, the misery
Lives lost, horrific costs—

shattered destinies.
No way to travel back in time
and return to where and when.
To just think "no" and save a friend.

Think about it…
To drive eyes wide open,
brain cells and fingertips all intact.
Prevent historical markers doomed with dread,
tallies of the dead…no need to travel back.
Or else, apologies not accepted—
epitaphs emotionally encrypted.

Think about it…
We want to live, laugh, love,
not crash, burn—cry and die.
Survive, thrive, and save lives, not kill.
AND STILL…
Will warnings halt the misery?
Will self-control happen and change deadly reality?

OTHER BOOKS BY THE AUTHOR

Gail (Davis) Galvan
(Pen names used at times)

On the Literary Road with a Writer (2014/revised 2015)

Sneezing Seasons 2013: The Inside Story about Allergies and Immunology (2013)

New Jack Rabbit City: Starring the Chicago Hares (with a co-author 2013, revised 2014)

A Nonviable Option: Suicide? Not! (2012)

Self-Publishing Sucks Sometimes and Here's Why (But Don't Give Up!) (2008)

Autoimmunity Counterattack: A Sequel/The Healthy Road Back (2005)

Autoimmunity Counterattack (2003)

Author Unknown, Author Undaunted (2003)

Affinity for Rainbows (2002 Edition)

Paycheck to Paycheck: Pre and Post Millennium Style (2000)

In Parents We Trust (2000)

OTHER BOOKS BY THE AUTHOR (con't)

Autobiography of an Allergic/Asthmatic Survivor (2001 and 2014 editions)

Sneezing Seasons (1999)

Books with other poets/writers:

Banta's Batter: Senior Savory Recipes and Merry Memories (2015)

*Poetry Palace: Boys and Girls Clubs (2010)

Poetry Palace (2005)

HS-Hoosier Storybook (2004)

HS-Hoosier Storybook (2002)

*Author's Note: No affiliation with Boys and Girls Clubs of America

To contact author:

Email: ggpodbooks@hotmail.com

Phone: 1-219-462-4422

Author's Websites:

www.gailgalvanbooks.today

www.gailgalvanbooks.com

www.newjackrabbitcity.com

For the *New Jack Rabbit City* fairy tale trailer:

https://www.youtube.com/watch?v=OIx83oIw76A&feature=youtu.be

Made in the USA
Charleston, SC
08 May 2016